Nightmare Island

Nightmare
Island *by* RON ROY

illustrated by Robert MacLean

A Unicorn Book · E. P. Dutton · New York

Library of Congress Cataloging in Publication Data

Roy, Ron, date   Nightmare Island.
(A Unicorn book)

Summary: On their first solo camping trip to Little
Island off the coast of Maine, Harley and his younger
brother are engulfed by a mysterious fire that starts
in the water and moves onto the island.
[1. Camping—Fiction. 2. Fires—Fiction.
3. Survival—Fiction. 4. Brothers and sisters—Fiction]
I. Mac Lean, Robert, date.   II. Title.
PZ7.R8139Ni [Fic] 80-23526 ISBN: 0-525-35905-2

Published in the United States by E. P. Dutton, a Division
of Elsevier-Dutton Publishing Company, Inc., New York

Published simultaneously in Canada by Clarke,
Irwin & Company Limited, Toronto and Vancouver

Editor: Emilie McLeod   Designer: Emily Sper

Printed in the U.S.A.   First Edition
10 9 8 7 6 5 4 3 2 1

for Chris and Ricky Lockwood,
whose uncle wishes
he could see them more often

Contents

1

Camping Out

The silver lure soared into the air, arched, and dropped, smacking the water.

"Beautiful cast, Harley," his father said as Harley reeled in. "Much better than I did at your age. Want to try a few with my new reel?"

"Thanks." What's he up to this time? thought Harley as they switched rods.

"Remember when you were Scoop's age and kept getting the line all balled up?" his father asked.

"Yeah, I remember." Here it comes, thought Harley.

"You sure were happy when your cousin Warren showed you how to release your thumb properly, remember? Warren must have been just about your age now, wasn't he?"

"I guess so," muttered Harley, thinking, he's closing in.

"Nice to have someone older to help you and teach you stuff when you're a kid," his father said, making a perfect cast with Harley's old rod.

"Dad?"

"Yes, son?"

"What do you want me to teach Scoopie?"

"Well, Scoop's been bugging your mom and me to let him go camping overnight on Little Island out there, and . . ."

Harley was caught. His father always knew just how to make him do something without really asking.

Harley let his lure rest in the water before beginning to reel it back. A water-skier's boat screamed in the evening stillness.

His father might have read Harley's thoughts. "I'm sorry this has been a slow summer for you, Harley. Doc Thatcher says if you take care of your elbow all summer, he'll let you back on skis this winter."

"Great," Harley said, reeling in. But would the summer ever end?

Two days after trying out his dad's new reel, Harley was taking his nine-year-old brother camping. Little Island was a quarter of a mile from Goose Island, where they had a summer house. It was visible from Goose Island, but too far to swim home from in case of an emergency. Harley was tuning up the 5½-horsepower motor on the aluminum skiff.

Harley brushed his sun-bleached hair out of his eyes and looked up. Scoop was dragging an overstuffed backpack out the door of the house. Harley turned back to the motor. Let him carry his own stupid pack, he thought. He was still annoyed that he'd gotten trapped into taking him camping.

"You look like a raccoon," Scoop said, dropping his pack on the dock beside Harley.

"What do you mean?"

"There's grease all around your eyes."

"How'd you like some?" Harley said, chasing Scoop back up the dock. They almost collided with their parents, who were coming to supervise the packing of the skiff.

"Harley, go wash your hands and face," his mother ordered.

"Honey, they're going camping, not out to dinner," her husband said. He winked at Harley and pretended to land a punch on his bad arm, the one he had broken playing spring ball. The arm kept him from water-skiing with his friends, but it let him take a nine-year-old kid camping.

"You guys all packed?" Harley's father asked. "Got the candy? Got the comics? Don't want to forget anything important, you know."

Harley grinned. He wished his dad was coming along on this trip. He'd even asked his father to come, but he was turned down. "Going camping with your older brother means a lot to a little guy, Harley," his dad had said. "This one's for Scoop."

Baby-sitting had never been Harley's idea of a good time. "Besides," his father had added, "your mother and I are going to beat Mr. and Mrs. Scoler in bridge tonight."

His mother looked worried. "Do you have your first-aid kit, flashlights and toothbrushes?"

Harley almost said they even had candles and matches, until he remembered: no fires. What good was camping without a fire? He'd already buried a bag of marshmallows at the bottom of his pack. Now he shoved the matches deeper into his back pocket.

Finally they were ready. Life vests on; tent, sleeping bags, packs, and cooler full of food in the boat. A kiss for Scoop and a hug for Harley.

"Don't stay up too late."

"Have a good time, you monkeys. See you tomorrow afternoon."

"Good luck in the bridge game."

The outboard sputtered to life and the boys were heading for Little Island. Harley, steering with his back to his parents, watched Little Island grow slowly bigger.

Scoop sat in the bow, facing Harley. He kept his eyes on his parents until they became specks in the distance.

2

Little Island

Harley maneuvered the skiff toward a small, sandy beach he'd noticed once while fishing. He nosed in, killed the motor. In the sudden silence he heard the keel strike sand. Scoop jumped out and tied the bow line to a tree while Harley threw the anchor aft.

"Leave the stuff in the boat till we find a campsite," Harley said.

They hiked in, and were swallowd up by towering pine trees and shoulder-high bushes. Little flecks of sunlight pierced the thick growth, but Harley shivered in the coolness.

"It's kind of spooky," Scoop whispered.

7

"Maybe we'll find a bloodthirsty pirate's treasure."

"The only thing we'll find is bloodthirsty mosquitoes," Harley said, smacking one on his neck.

Near the southwest edge of the island, they found a small clearing. Tall pine trees formed a circle around it, and their needles made its soft carpet. A fire-blackened rock showed that someone else had liked this spot, too.

"How about it?" Scoop asked. They agreed quickly, which was unusual. They both wanted to start exploring, and in two trips they had all their gear in the clearing.

They pitched the tent first. It was a light, two-man pup tent, which went up easily. "It's like a pocket," explained Harley. "When it's all zipped up, nothing can get in. I'll go inside and put up the poles. You stay outside and pound in the stakes on all the corners."

"Okay, Harl."

"And be careful of the hatchet; it's sharp."

"Right."

With Harley holding the poles in place while Scoop pounded the stakes, the bright orange tent was up in two minutes. "Okay, now drive the stakes in further. I don't want this thing collapsing on my head tonight."

Scoop did as he was told. Driving stakes

through pine needles, he discovered, was easy. Too easy. Quickly the stakes disappeared, and the rope loops slipped off the tops. The tension of the front guy rope pulled the tent forward, and the rear collapsed.

Harley was inside yelling, *"Scoopie, what in blazes are you doing?"*

"I just pounded in the stakes, Harl, like you—"

"Get me out of here!"

"How?"

"Unzip the zipper, dummy. It's hot in here."

Harley came out, mad. "This time I'll do the stakes and you go inside. Give me the hatchet."

Scoop crawled inside the deflated tent. "Now what do I do?"

"Stick the pointy ends of the poles through those little metal things in the roof." Harley looked around for the tent stakes. "Where are the stakes, Scoop?"

Silence from inside the tent. Then Scoop said, "I think they're buried in the ground."

"Great," Harley muttered. But he found them, and soon the tent was up again, taut and mosquito-proof. They dragged small logs into the clearing for seats, and hung their life vests and backpacks on tree branches.

When they were finished, the campsite looked

like a drawing from a scout manual. They even had a small table.

"You can't just put your food on the *ground*!" their mother had declared, loading the table into the skiff. "Aren't there mice or something out there?"

This had gotten a hilarious laugh from everyone.

"No, mom, just bears," Harley had teased.

"They won't eat you two," their father had quipped. "I read somewhere they don't like dirt."

When Scoop and Harley were satisfied that their camp was comfortable, they set out to see the rest of the island. With no direction in mind, they followed their noses into the underbrush.

Scoop saw it first. "Look, Harl—a cave in those rocks!"

The cave turned out to be no more than a crevice between two tall boulders. Located on the only high ground, the rocks were visible from all parts of the island.

"Neat place for a lookout," Scoop said. "Let's climb up." The rocks were broad at the bottom and narrower at the top, like two flatirons leaning against each other. Harley's elbow made the climb difficult, but within minutes they were both standing at the top.

"What a view!" Scoop cried. "Look, there's Goose Island and the mainland."

The twenty islands in the cluster where the Evans family had their summer house were no more than rock outcroppings. The larger ones had homes on them, but even the smallest islands were used by picnickers. The older kids liked the less popular islands for dates in the family boats.

It was hot on top of the rocks. Harley turned to find the ocean breeze. "Look, Scoop, a shark!"

"Where?"

Harley pointed straight out to sea. He was kidding, but there *was* a black something on the horizon.

"That's no shark," Scoop said. "But what is it? It's not an island."

They watched, hands shielding their eyes. "Not moving," Harley said. "Must be an island." Then, quickly bored, he began sliding back to the ground. "Let's get some food."

Scoop used toe- and handholds, and Harley was down first. "Race you to the tent!" he yelled. With his head start, Harley easily crashed his way through the underbrush ahead of his brother. When Scoop got to the campsite, Harley was already popping cookies into his mouth.

"Save some for me, Harl," Scoop said.

Reluctantly, Harley tossed him the bag. Having a nine-year-old brother is a pain, he thought.

For eight years Harley had enjoyed the privileges of the only child. Meals had been planned around his likes. All the toys had been his alone. He'd had his own bedroom in the city apartment. Then one day his parents had told him they were planning to adopt a brother for him.

"Why?" Harley had asked.

"We want you to have someone to play with," his mother had answered.

"How old is he?"

"We don't really know yet," they'd said. And gradually Harley had grown used to the idea. It might be neat having a brother my age, he'd thought.

Then they'd brought home this little tiny kid. He was three years old.

Harley had been disappointed and resentful. It took a year before he began to pay any attention to Scoop. And then it was only because they moved him in to share Harley's room. From then on it was "Save some for me, Harl" and "Can I come with you, Harl?" Sharing was still not one of Harley's best points.

Millie Evans knew her sons well. She had packed enough food for four boys. There were six sandwiches for each, with a choice of ham and cheese, tuna, or peanut butter and jelly; there were two quarts of milk, one white and one chocolate, and a box of cereal; there was half a chocolate cake; and of course raisins, chips, fruit and cookies. The Evans boys might get dirty and mosquito-bitten, but starve they would not.

Harley had hoped for hot dogs over a fire, but that had been settled early. Camping yes, but no fires. Period. Harley had mumbled agreement, then helped himself to some matches.

By the time the island had been thoroughly explored and half the cake and sandwiches eaten, it was getting dark. Lights from the larger islands were visible from the shore near the rocks. "Which one's Goose Island?" Scoop asked, confused by the growing darkness.

"There," said Harley, pointing. The Goose Island summer residents had their houses near the water. A clubhouse had been built in some pines. The lights of this building shone like a beacon to Harley and Scoop.

"What do you think mom and dad are doing right now?" Scoop asked.

"Probably beating the pants off Mr. and Mrs. Scoler in bridge," Harley answered.

"You mean they'll have to play in their underwear?"

"Under where?" said Harley, which struck them both as the funniest thing they'd ever heard. Only a gull heard the laughter and saw the two boys rolling in the sand, clutching at their sides.

When the gasps and hiccups stopped, they groped their way back to the campsite and into the tent. After a few minutes of peeling off jeans and socks, and bumping heads in the dark, they settled into their sleeping bags.

"Harl?"

Harley grunted and rolled away from his brother's muffled voice.

"Thanks for coming with me, Harl."

Harley didn't say anything.

"Good night, Harl."

Soon they were both asleep.

3

Fire

Harley sat up in his sleeping bag. Something had awakened him. He lay back, listening. Finally, he crawled out of his bag and peeked through the mesh door of the tent. His heart was thudding, but he saw only blackness and heard only silence.

He slipped on his jeans, T-shirt, and sneakers. Scoop mumbled in his sleep as Harley left the tent, hoping he wouldn't meet a skunk. Or a bear. But there was nothing except tree giants in the darkness. And mosquitoes.

He pulled the book of matches from his pocket, struck one, and looked at his watch. Twelve-thirty. He'd been asleep for a little over three hours. Now he was wide awake. And hungry.

He found his backpack where he'd hung it on a branch. The marshmallows were squashed. Like to roast some of these, he thought. Then he remembered his parents' orders about fires. But who's going to tell? I'm probably the only person awake for miles, he told himself.

His eyes had grown accustomed to the darkness, and he had no trouble finding firewood. He decided to build the fire near the water on the shore facing out to sea, away from Goose Island. No sense in taking any chances of being seen.

Dry pine needles first, then small twigs; bigger twigs next, then some small branches. The flames lit up Harley's face, warming it. The fire felt good. Maybe I should wake Scoop, he thought. But what if he squealed to mom? Then Harley remembered how Scoop had thanked him last night.

Should he leave the fire? It was on the sand of the cove, five feet from the water, but only about three feet from grass and bushes. And they were dry from the August sun. Harley circled the fire with rocks, then went to wake Scoop.

In the tent, he thumped the sleeping bag where he thought Scoop's rear end should be.

"Scoop, wake up, it's me. I've got a fire going for marshmallows. Come on."

Scoop sat up. "Marshmallows? But mom said we couldn't have a fire."

"All right, go back to sleep and I'll eat them all myself," Harley said, backing out of the tent.

"Wait, I'm coming!" Scoop said. He kicked his way out of the sleeping bag and thrashed around for his clothes.

Harley waited outside the tent in the dark, finishing the chocolate cake. He could just see the glow of the fire flickering through the trees. All around him crickets were winding up the evening's chorus.

"Where is it?" Scoop whispered, emerging from the tent.

"Follow me." Harley led the way through the darkness. The giant trees and thick bushes made walking in the dark rough, but the glow of the fire gave them a direction.

"Neat!" Scoop cried when they walked out of the undergrowth onto the beach. He looked like an Indian as he knelt and put his hands near the flames. It had burned low while Harley was gone. He tossed more branches on as Scoop tore open the marshmallows.

"We need some sticks, Harl."

They found a sapling at the edge of the woods and removed two thin branches. Harley

18

made clean cuts near the trunk, as his father had shown him. He sharpened the ends of the sticks, gave one to Scoop and impaled a fat marshmallow on his own.

Scoop ate his first one right out of the bag. "If mom saw this fire, she'd kill us," he mumbled around a mouthful of marshmallow.

"She's not going to see it," Harley said. "And she's not going to hear about it, either."

"I won't tell."

"Good. I won't either."

The boys gobbled the marshmallows as if they

hadn't seen food in a week. Scoop had goo in his eyebrows as well as all around his mouth. Harley lay back in the sand and burped.

With some difficulty, they finished the whole bag. Scoop had to force himself to eat his last. "I think I'm going to throw up," he moaned.

"Me too," Harley said. He stood, patted his belly and tossed his stick into the fire. "Come on, let's wash our hands. This stuff is sticky."

They squatted at the edge of the water and splashed the stickiness from their fingers and faces.

"Harl, look, something's out there!"

They stared, trying to see what it was, if it was moving, if it was coming toward Little Island.

"Looks like a big ship," said Harley.

"Why doesn't it have any lights?"

"Maybe they don't want anyone to know they're out there," Harley said, lowering his voice.

"Why not?" Scoop asked.

"Because they're pirates," Harley answered, his voice a menacing whisper.

"What do pirates want in Maine?"

"They want to kidnap nine-year-old boys and *eat them*!"

"Come on, Harl, don't kid around."

Harley laughed and finished washing his

fingers. "Tide's coming in," he said, wiping his hands on his jeans.

"How do you know?"

"Simple—the water's closer to the fire than when I lit it. And the wind's coming up. Dad says you can always tell when the tide is starting to come in because of the breeze that comes with it."

"What's that smell?" Scoop said, sniffing his fingers.

"What smell?"

"Something smells funny, on my hands."

"Pollution, probably," Harley answered. "Dad says in five or ten years it won't be safe to eat the fish anymore."

"When I grow up I'm going to help save the ocean like Jacques Cousteau."

"How can you save the ocean if you can't even remember to brush your teeth?" Harley teased.

"Come on, Harl," Scoop said, embarrassed.

"Just kidding, Scoopie. I didn't even bring my toothbrush with me."

"You didn't? Good, me either."

They were sitting by the fire again. Scoop yawned, making Harley yawn. Then they yawned together.

"How're we going to put the fire out?" Scoop asked.

Harley glanced around in the shadows, but saw nothing for carrying water. "Bury it," he said, kicking sand into the flames. "Except for this." He picked up a branch as big around as his arm. One end was burning, but the other hadn't been in the flames at all. Stepping close to the water, he leaned back and flung the branch as far as he could into the black ocean.

He heard it splash, then turned back to kick more sand over the fire.

The noise came first. A *WHOOSH* so loud it shook them. The sea burst into flames that shot thirty feet into the night. Both boys whirled around as what had been a dark sea became an inferno of flames.

"Harl! What happened?" Scoop's eyes were mirrors, reflecting terror.

Harley's mouth went dry. The hairs on the back of his neck stood out straight.

"The ocean is on fire," he whispered.

4

Inside the Circle

The boys stared in horror as smoke and fire billowed into the night with a roar. The flames shot up fifty feet from where they stood, forcing them to back away.

As they watched, unbelieving, the fire spread. They saw the flames eat along the surface of the water to the right and left of where Harley had thrown the burning branch.

Harley's breath came in gasps. He knew something was in the water, and it was the something Scoop had smelled. He also knew that the tide and the winds were spreading the fire.

"What'll we do, Harl?" Scoop's question cut into Harley's fear.

"The boat! We've got to get to the boat!" They raced along the shore, crashing through bushes and small trees. Harley was aware that the fire in the water was also racing. He and the fire were racing to the boat, their only way of getting off the island.

Harley and Scoop stopped, breathless, when they reached the spot where the boat was tied. The fire had kept up with them.

"We're cut off!" Harley screamed above the

roar of the fire. "It's going all around the island! We'll never get the boat through!"

"What are we going to do?" Scoop asked. His face was orange in the glare. The heat made him squint like a Halloween pumpkin.

"Get the boat away from the water so the fire can't get at the motor!" Harley yelled. "We'll have to wait it out; a lot of people will see the fire and come to help."

Harley knew he was talking more to make

Scoop feel better than because he had any faith in what he was saying. He wished he could go back to sleep and wake up again. No marshmallows, no fire, no burning sea.

Scoop's hands shook as he began untying the knots he'd tied only a few hours ago.

Harley splashed toward the stern. "I'll get this one." He freed the anchor line, then, straining, lifted the stern of the boat and the motor. He felt pain in his elbow, but heard the crackle of the fire like jeers at his back.

"Pull!" he yelled to Scoop at the bow, silently thanking his dad for refusing to let them take the heavy Whaler for this trip. With Scoop's help, Harley shoved the aluminum boat out of the water. Then, one foot after another, lifting, pushing, dragging, they moved it into the bushes above the sand.

Behind Harley, the fire lit the night. His back stung with the feeling he had after skiing when he put his rear too close to the fireplace. Was it his imagination, or was the fire closer to the island?

"Where are we taking it?" Scoop asked, still pulling at the bow.

"Near the tent. Stay along the edge till we get closer to the campsite. We'd never get it through all those trees!"

In spite of the added weight of the small

motor and gas tank, they were able to carry and slide the skiff through the short bushes along the shore. Where there was grass, they slid the boat on its bottom. Harley wasn't sure how far they should go before leaving the shore to find the camp. The fire lit the bank like streetlights, but the rest of the island was deep in shadow.

The boys kept their eyes on the fire as they dragged the boat. As far as they could see in any direction, smoke and flames were filling the night. They were in the middle of a burning circle. Only a few yards of water were not yet covered with flames.

"I see it, through those two big trees," Scoop said suddenly. Harley peered into the dim woods. "I think I see something," Scoop added.

He was right. They were only twenty feet from the tent; but they had to carry the boat now, over the thick bushes that grew inland.

They were both out of breath when they dropped the boat and collapsed on the ground. Neither said anything for a few minutes. They sat staring at the fire visible through the trees.

"Harl, what started the fire? Water can't burn."

"That smell must have been oil or something on the water; it'll burn if something starts it off," Harley answered, still dazed by the sight of the fire.

"Was it the stick you threw?"

Harley didn't answer. Suddenly he was on his feet, moving.

"What's the matter?" Scoop asked.

"A tree's on fire!" Harley cried, crashing through the tent flaps. Then he was coming out, dragging the sleeping bags after him.

Then Scoop saw it too. A tree, long dead and hanging over the water, was burning. Its dry branches held drier needles. Pitch ooze, gelled by time, clung to the bark. The whole thing was a fuse which would bring the fire into the bushes that grew near it.

"Come on!" Harley raced to the tree, throwing both bags into the water. Hoping there was no oil there, he dragged his sopping bag through the water to the burning tree and flopped it over the flames.

Scoop was having trouble wrestling his bag out of the water. "It's too heavy, I can't carry it!"

"Then drag it," Harley shouted. "We can't let the fire spread!"

Harley was knee-deep in water. He slapped at the burning branches with one end of the soaked bag. Giving up on his, Scoop came and splashed with his hands.

"Harl, another one's on fire!" Harley whipped around. Twenty yards away another tree was burning like a giant torch. The boys stared, not believing. The fire in the water was now on the island.

Harley yanked his sleeping bag off the tree trunk and climbed to dry land. "Come on, let's get out of here!" Scoop followed, leaving his bag floating in the water.

At the campsite, Harley dropped his wet sleeping bag on the ground. Then he saw the boat motor and gas tank, still attached to the skiff. "Help me get these off before the fire gets here!"

The boys scraped knuckles and bumped heads in their panic to loosen the bolts. Finally, the motor came free, and they laid it on its side. Gas oozed into the pine needles.

"Away from the tent!" Harley yelled. "Grab the tank!"

They dragged the motor and tank through the bushes and trees, dripping gas as they went. Harley cursed himself. If he had thought ahead even one minute, he would have known enough to leave the motor and tank at the water's edge in the first place. But he couldn't think ahead. He could hardly think at all. Now they were using up precious minutes.

They reached another small cove. To the right, the two dead trees still burned. Since the water in this cove was not burning, Harley took a chance that there was no oil near the shore. He dumped the motor into the shallows.

"Throw in the tank," he ordered when they reached the closest point on the shore.

"Won't it burn," asked Scoop, "like the oil?"

"Throw it in, damn it!" Harley screamed. "We have to get rid of it!"

He ran to help Scoop. Together they tossed the gas tank into the water. It floated, like some half-filled toy in a bathtub.

Something told Scoop they had just thrown away their only chance of leaving the island. He began sobbing, slowly at first; then, bent at the waist, he threw up his supper.

Harley was in shock. He could not make a decision; panic prevented any thought from entering his mind. The roaring sound in the sea was coming closer. And he could smell smoke.

He went to Scoop and put an arm across his back. He felt Scoop shuddering from sobs and retching. "Scoop, don't cry; it's going to be all right. We'll figure something out, okay?"

Holding hands, they ran back to the campsite. Harley flopped to the ground, but Scoop stood above him.

"What are we going to do?" he asked. His face was white.

Harley knew Scoop was depending on him. He had to do something, anything, if only to keep his brother from panicking. He stood and looked into the trees that surrounded the camp-site. A few bushes along the shore had caught fire from the burning trees. As the sea wind blew across the island, more trees and bushes would catch. Nothing would stop the fire from spreading through the whole island.

"Find dad's shovel," Harley said hoarsely.

Harley felt paralyzed, as in one of those dreams where the horror is coming for you and you're unable to move. He shook himself, took the shovel and tried to dig through the pine needles. "We'll dig a hole, cover ourselves with dirt." Immediately his shovel struck something hard. Rocks. He tried another spot, then another. There were rocks everywhere. He let the shovel fall from his hands.

Scoop watched, in a trance. "Where's your sleeping bag?" Harley asked.

"I left it in the water. It was too heavy."

"Get it. We'll wrap ourselves in the wet bags and crawl under the boat. It's our only chance."

Harley helped Scoop retrieve his bag, then zipped him into it to the waist. He did the same with his own bag, so that both had their arms free.

They crawled over to the boat and lay next to it. Lifting one side, they dragged the boat till it was directly over their bodies.

Then they lowered it, and they were inside.

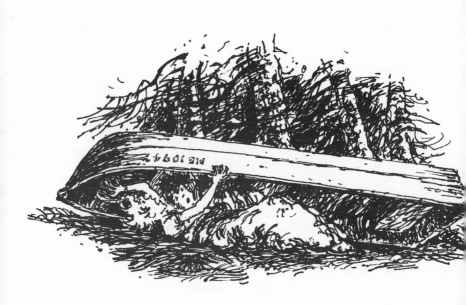

5

Outside the Circle

Mildred Evans was awake. She wondered what time it was, but her wristwatch was on the bureau. She groped for her husband's wrist, but he was lying on it. Then she lay back and tried to figure out what had waked her.

Maybe I'm still tense from the bridge game, she thought. Smiling, she remembered the long, drawn-out final rubber. And her husband's winning six no-trump bid. The game had broken up at midnight. It was then that they'd all seen the flare in the sky and wondered if some boat were in trouble. The flare had died out and there hadn't been a second one.

Finally she swung her legs out of bed and tiptoed to her bureau to look at her watch.

She screamed. Just stood there, screaming. The mirror was afire with reflected flames.

Her husband jumped out of his sleep. "What's the matter?"

"Fire! There's a fire somewhere!" By then she had crossed to the window. "It's Little Island! Peter, the boys!" She was screaming and trying to find clothes at the same time.

Her husband found the phone and dialed O. "This is Peter Evans on Goose Island. There's a fire on one of the islands near us. We think it's Little Island, and our sons are out there camping. Please call the police and the fire department. Hurry!"

Millie was pulling sneakers on, unable to take her eyes from the window. Her husband was yanking pants on over his pajama bottoms, hopping from one foot to the other.

"Let's go."

They ran down the stairs, out the back door, and raced for the dock.

Their neighbors, having heard the screams, were on their porch. "Millie, Peter, what is it? What's burning?"

"Fire on Little Island," Peter cried. "The boys are camping out there—can you help?"

"My God! What can we do?" they asked.

"Tell the others. Bring extinguishers, blankets, anything!"

Peter inserted the key into the Whaler ignition. The motor coughed, sputtered, then died. He tried again. More coughs. Again it sputtered out.

"Come on!" he screamed at the motor.

"Hurry, Peter!"

"I am! I think I've flooded it." Slowly, Peter, he told himself. Don't panic. Pull the choke, just a little. Now turn the key. It caught, roared into life. Peter wiped the sweat from his forehead.

"Hang on!" he shouted to his wife, who was sitting in the bow. Her fingers were clamped to the gunwales, showing white knuckles.

Ahead of them, the night was orange. Flames climbed into the night over an area the size of two football fields. Black smoke blotted out the stars.

Millie stared at the horror. She would have swum if that would have gotten her there faster. The boat slowed suddenly, dipping the bow. "What is it, Peter?" she asked in the sudden quiet.

"Look," he said, pointing. Where Little Island should have been, flames were shooting straight out of the water. "The water's burning," Peter said, amazed. From where he sat he could not tell if the island was burning as well.

"What can we do?" Millie asked.

"I can't go any closer," he said. Then he changed his mind. They couldn't just sit there. "Maybe there's a way through!"

The engine roared and the Whaler surged forward again. Peter wondered what he would do if he did find a way to get through the burning maze. Would he take it, and risk the motor's exploding, killing Millie and himself . . . ? He never finished his thought. Suddenly the night and the whole world exploded. The noise came first. Then a ball of fire shot into the sky from somewhere in front of them. It lit the sky and sent burning debris flying into the night.

"Oh my God!" shrieked Millie. "What is it, Peter? *What is it?*"

"Something exploded," he shouted over the noise. He felt his hands shaking. Please God, let it be far from the boys.

The sound of a siren pierced through the noise of roaring fire. Searchlights swept the black water.

"Fireboats!" Peter cried.

Moments later, three large boats came out of the night. They slowed and stopped one hundred feet from the fire. Peter gunned the Whaler and moved alongside one of the boats. Against the light of the flames a Coast Guard launch was silhouetted.

36

"Our two sons are on an island in the middle of the fire!" he shouted up at an officer. "What can we do? We have to get in there!"

"Can't get in," the officer yelled back. "Burning oil, a slick of some kind. That was a tanker just blew up!"

"But what about the island? Is Little Island burning too?"

"Can't tell from here—too much smoke. Have to wait for the fireboats to smother some of this.

We'll try to get a helicopter to take your boys out." Then the big boat was gone, leaving the Whaler rocking in its wake.

A small boat sidled up to the Whaler. "Peter, what on earth has happened?" It was the Scolers, partly dressed in nightclothes, partly in foul-weather gear.

"We don't know exactly," Peter said. "It's an oil slick; something exploded."

"We saw it," Ray Scoler said. "What about the island? Is there any way . . . ?"

"The fireboats are trying to put it out," Peter said. "We'll have to wait a little longer; they're calling for a helicopter."

Bertha Scoler looked at Millie sitting in the bow. Her face was white, even in the glow of the fire. Her eyes strained to see through the smoke and flames.

"Millie, it will be all right."

Millie didn't hear her friend's words over the noise of the boats. Her mind was on Little Island, with her sons. She had given them permission to go camping, and had helped them pack the boat. "Oh God, help them," she cried, the tears sliding down her face.

6

Harley's Decision

Harley was suffocating. The boat's middle seat was pressed against his stomach, making it difficult to breathe. The bow seat was only two inches above his forehead. Scoop was crushed up against his left shoulder.

"Harl, I'm hot."

"Me too. It's only the sleeping bags; the fire's not here yet, Scoop." *Yet.* How long till it gets here? he wondered.

"How long will we have to—?" Scoop never finished his question. Suddenly the island, the earth, the universe exploded. The ground under the boys trembled; the force of the blast slamming against the boat made their ears ring.

Scoop screamed and Harley bumped his head as he jerked in fright. Then it was quiet, except for the growing whispers of burning wood.

"Wh-what was that?" Scoop asked. His voice sounded far away, even though his mouth was inches from Harley's ear.

"Something exploded." Harley had gone from sweltering hot to shivering cold in seconds. He heard his heart pounding.

"Harl, remember that big boat we saw? Do you think that's where the oil came from?"

"Probably." Harley's head was beginning to ache. He couldn't believe he was lying under a boat in the middle of a burning island.

"Maybe it was—"

"Shut up. Listen!" It sounded like fingernails on a blackboard. It got louder, then something crashed. They felt the thud as whatever it was fell near the boat.

Harley waited, holding his breath. Finally he breathed, instantly gagging on smoke. Tears streamed down his face into his ears.

"What's the matter?" Scoop asked.

"I think a tree fell," Harley answered, coughing. "It must be on my side of the boat. The smoke is coming right under!" He was trying to keep his voice under control. He failed. He felt like throwing the boat off and running. But where would he run?

He knew more trees would fall. Dozens of giant old pines surrounded the campsite. Any one of them could crush the skiff like a walnut. They'd have to move. But there was no place to go.

"Scoop, listen. We can't stay under the boat."

"Where can we go?" Scoop sounded as if he wanted to cry, but he wouldn't. For Harl.

"I don't know; maybe somewhere in the water." Harley's mind was racing, trying to think of possibilities he'd overlooked.

"In the water? But what about the fire?"

"There might be a place where there's no oil," Harley said. "Let's lift the boat a little so I can see out."

Both boys placed their hands on the floor of the boat and lifted. "Not too much," Harley warned. With the skiff ten inches off the ground, they stopped.

The burning tree lay four feet from Harley's face. Smoke poured into the opening. Both boys coughed, and covered their mouths and noses with one hand. Their eyes stung and tears washed down their faces.

The ocean fire, just visible through the trees, raged on. All around the campsite, island vegetation burned. They heard the crackling even where they did not yet see fire. Harley knew it was spreading fast. It would reach them soon. The campsite should have been burning already, he thought. The wind must have shifted. But they couldn't stay here. Bushes, pine needles, their gear, everything would burn.

Scoop wiped the tears from his eyes. Smoke crept across the ground like fog. "Harl, look, the rocks!"

Harley was on the wrong side of the boat. "I can't see them from here."

"There's no fire up there," Scoop said. "Maybe we can hide there!"

Harley tried to picture the rocks. He couldn't remember. "Help me lift the boat higher." They pushed and turned the boat until it stood straight, balanced on its side by Harley.

More smoke swirled over them. "Don't take deep breaths!" Harley shouted. The tops of some of the surrounding trees were burning like huge torches. Bushes burned wherever the wind had tossed sparks. Everywhere the boys looked they saw flames and smoke.

"Over there," Scoop said, trying not to breathe. The rocks they had stood on only hours ago loomed in the glare of the fire like huge hands folded in prayer. Where the thumbs should be, a narrow depression was hidden in shadow.

Smoke, carried by the wind, blew across the rocks. They were barely visible, then completely hidden.

Harley wiped his eyes. Were the rocks really there at all? Everything seemed like a nightmare. Scoop started coughing violently. "Take off your shirt," Harley yelled. "Use it to cover your face."

"Can we hide between the rocks?" Scoop asked, pulling off his shirt.

"I don't think the hole is big enough."

"But you said we can't stay here!" Scoop's voice was thin, near hysteria.

Harley felt desperate. He swung his eyes to the woods around them. He wanted to see a magic tunnel that would lead them through the fire. But there was no magic tunnel. And he knew that trying to escape the fire by running into the water was a stupid idea. The sea all around the island was a furnace.

They'd have to try for the rocks. If they stayed under the boat, they could be crushed. Or suffocated. Harley looked at the rocks again. They were about one hundred yards from the skiff. Half those yards were covered with burning trees and bushes.

Harley felt sick. His headache was making him nauseous. He swallowed, tasting smoke and sweat. He shoved the boat onto its keel and stood up. The wet sleeping bag slid to his ankles.

"Come on, Scoop. We're going for the rocks."

Scoop sat huddled in his wet bag. He looked shrunken, like a little old man. The light on his face made his eyes sink in shadow. "Through the fire?" he asked.

Harley stepped out of his sleeping bag. "Through the fire," he answered.

7

Through the Fire

Harley shook the contents of his pack onto the ground. "Get the flashlight," he ordered Scoop. "And the canteen of water."

While Scoop looked, Harley opened his jackknife. Without a pause, he slashed the bottom out of his sleeping bag. Zipped, it would be a tube open at both ends. He did the same to Scoop's bag. With his T-shirt tied around his face, he looked like a vandal crazily slashing out his anger.

"Mom will kill you!" Scoop said when he saw what Harley had done.

"Got the flashlight?"

"I can't find it," Scoop said. "But I saw it somewhere."

"Look in the tent, and hurry up!" Harley looked up at the burning treetops. What if another tree decided to fall across the campsite right now? He shivered.

Scoop backed out of the tent with the flashlight in his hand.

"Take off your belt," Harley said. He removed his own, and when he had Scoop's, he tied them together at the pointy ends. Using his knife, he cut holes in both sleeping bags. Then he stuck a belt buckle through each hole.

"Okay, climb into your sleeping bag," Harley said. "Your feet will stick out so you can walk." Harley hung the canteen around his neck by the strap. By its weight he thought it must be almost full. He jammed the flashlight and knife into pockets.

"Hold on to the belt so we don't lose each other. Can you walk all right?"

Scoop took a few steps. By holding the bag off the ground from inside, he was able to move his feet without tripping. In the shadows made by the fire, he looked like some giant larva wriggling inside its cocoon. "It's okay," he said.

Harley zipped Scoop's bag up as far as it would go. Then he tied the drawstring around his neck so the bag wouldn't slip down. With a sudden inspiration, he unscrewed the canteen top and poured water over Scoop's hair. Then he did the same to himself.

He slipped his wet sleeping bag over his head and shoulders. It was cold and clammy.

When Harley's bag was zipped, the boys shuffled away from the campsite with Harley in the lead. Fire was visible through the trees in every direction, spreading even faster than Harley had imagined.

"It's like a sack race." Scoop giggled nervously.

Harley stopped. Fire was directly ahead of him. He shielded his eyes from the heat and glare. Looking up, he could just make out the form of the rocks though the smoke and flames.

Suddenly he knew it was all hopeless. The sleeping bags, the water on their heads. For nothing. He couldn't lead his brother into those flames. He turned and looked at Scoop's scared eyes. Scoop was ready for whatever Harley thought was right. Oh God, thought Harley. Make this be right.

He stared into the flames. Was there a way through? Sure the sleeping bags covered their bodies, but what about their faces? And how long would their sneakers keep their feet from burning? Harley had to take the chance that they could get through fifty yards of burning trees and bushes fast enough. If they got caught in the middle, or lost . . . He stopped thinking. Move, Harl, he told himself.

Marking a straight line in his mind's eye, he was ready. He tugged on the belt clenched in his sweaty fist. "Okay?" he yelled over his shoulder.

Scoop tugged back. Ready. Hunching their shoulders, they walked into the flames.

"Don't drop the belt!" Harley yelled.

The heat smacked them like a wave of boiling water. Harley staggered from the impact, but kept walking. Using shoulders and knees as bumpers, he shoved burning branches out of their path. Their feet found a way over the ground, blindly searching out a path.

Progress was agonizingly slow. Harley could see only a few feet ahead of his face. Smoke was everywhere; his eyes, mouth, nose burned from it. He ached to take a deep breath, but knew he would gag and probably throw up if he did.

There were spaces between the big trees, room to walk through. They pushed through burning bushes. The wet bags sizzled and steamed and began to smell of scorched feathers. They kept moving.

Harley stopped once in a small clearing long enough to check his direction. The rocks were still straight ahead.

A sickening smell filled Harley's nostrils. It was scorched down. Or his hair. Wildly, he switched his end of the belts to his other hand and reached through the hole in the bag. His head felt hot, steaming. But his hair hadn't burned.

He kept moving. Tears and smoke half blinding him, he hunched his shoulders and squinted his eyes. One foot ahead of the other. Don't think. Walk.

Then it happened. Suddenly Harley's end of the belt was ripped from his hand. He whirled around and felt his heart stop.

Scoop was not there.

8

The Rocks

Harley wailed in horror. *"Scoop! Where are you?"* Half blinded by smoke, he screamed again. Then he saw him, a crumpled ball on the ground. His scream died in his throat.

He let his sleeping bag drop and leaped toward the motionless form. He grabbed Scoop and turned him over. His eyes were closed; a small cut was bleeding on his forehead. "Scoop, wake up! *Scoopie!"*

Panic clawed at the inside of his stomach. He wanted to vomit. He looked around wildly. The flames reared high, bright yellow on the edges, red and blue at the base. Suddenly, a *whoof* of

51

flame shot up at his side with a sound like tearing cloth. There was a gasp as fire took hold of another bush.

Harley grabbed Scoop by the shoulders. Could he carry him? Hands shaking with desperation, he poured the last of the water in the canteen over Scoop's face.

Scoop's eyelids fluttered, then slowly opened. The relief made Harley feel weak.

"Scoop, can you stand up? We have to keep going!" All around them he could hear the tearing, dreadful sound of flames in the undergrowth. He was aware of the smell too, more bitter than any bonfire.

Scoop stared at his brother. "What happened, Harl?"

"You must have tripped. Come on, I'll help you up."

When Scoop had his balance, Harley scuttled back into his sleeping bag. This time he held Scoop's hand through the holes in the bags. Shouldering his way through the wall of flames, he headed for the rocks.

The fire roared through trees, bushes, grass. Like a huge beast it raged, gobbling up anything in its greed. Flames licked at the boys' faces, singeing their hair. Sparks leaped at them, stinging their hands and faces. Their eyes teared from the smoke. But the wet bags worked.

The ground began to slope upward. When the boys walked out of the burning thicket, the rocks were straight ahead. Scoop stumbled, exhausted. Sweat ran down his smoke-blackened face in streams. His eyes were red slits from the smoke and sweat. He was sobbing with relief. So was Harley, now that the fire was behind them.

"Can't stop . . . have to keep going . . ." Harley gasped between snatches of breath. "Fire will be here soon. . . . Look."

Scoop looked where Harley pointed. The rocks stood higher than the rest of the island. There were trees, but not many. Shoulder-high bushes covered the ground thickly between where they stood and the rocks. The wind was still blowing across the island. Harley knew the bushes ahead of them would be ablaze in minutes. They had to get to the rocks before the fire did.

"Let's go!" Hitching their sleeping bags up to their hips, they pushed their way into the thick bushes. Brambles caught at their feet. Thorns ripped and shredded the bags. Sparks and smoke swirled around their heads. A rabbit shot out in front of them, running from the smoke.

Scoop fell to his knees. "I can't go any more!" he cried, choking on his own sobs.

Harley kneeled next to him. "It's only a few more feet. Look."

Scoop looked up, wiping his nose with the back of his hand. The rocks loomed directly in front of them. Tall, wrapped in shadows, they would have scared Scoop on any other night. Now they seemed welcoming.

Harley heard a crackling, like paper being crumpled in some unseen hand. He turned; the bushes they had just struggled through were beginning to burn. He jumped to his feet, dragging Scoop up with him. Holding on to each other, they ran, crawled to the rocks.

Huddled together, they crouched against the rocks, catching air in their lungs. In front of them, smoke swirled like a dark sea. The flames were a tidal wave with the power to sweep over and crush everything in its path. High above, unseen gulls screamed in angry fear.

With the rocks at their backs, they felt almost safe. But Harley saw the danger coming closer. The wind had spread the fire so that it formed a huge half circle. Now it was coming toward the rocks where they sat. He wanted to cry. There was no place left to run, even if they had the strength. It would be so much easier just to go to sleep here, leaning against the rocks. Let the fire come and get them.

Instead, he dragged himself to his feet. He saw the burning acre they'd just walked through. Beyond that, there was nothing but flames and smoke and swirling specks of char and ash.

Harley let his sleeping bag drop to his waist, and shivered in the night air. One wrist throbbed from a burn he didn't remember receiving. Several burns stung his face. He looked at Scoop. His hair was singed, and the cut on his forehead had swollen into a painful-looking lump. His face was black except for the eyes. Now who looks like a raccoon, Harley thought. "You okay?" he asked.

"I guess so," Scoop answered. His voice was hoarse, as though he'd been yelling for hours. He stared as the fire licked closer. "It's still coming," he whispered.

Suddenly Scoop whirled around to the rocks behind them. The look on his face told Harley that Scoop had just realized what he, Harley, had known all along. There was no cave in the rocks. A crack between the two boulders. A small depression at the bottom. Not room enough for two boys to escape a raging forest fire.

9

Alone

They stared at the crack in the rocks.

"How will we fit?" Scoop's voice was trembling. He looked behind them at the burning bushes, then turned back quickly.

"We won't," Harley answered. "But you will. I can squeeze in on the other side. Try to get in."

Scoop dropped to his knees, draped in the wet sleeping bag. He tried to fit into the space by crawling in frontwards. It was no use. His rear and legs stuck out behind him.

"Try it backwards!" Harley said sharply. The panic he felt made him impatient. But he knew it wasn't Scoop's fault, it was his. If he hadn't taken those matches, built the fire . . .

Scoop interrupted his thoughts. "If I sit on my feet and scrunch down, I can fit."

He was right. Facing out, with his legs under him, Scoop tucked right into the bottom of the crack, before it narrowed over his head and disappeared.

Harley knelt and yanked Scoop's sleeping bag up over his head so he was completely covered. He pulled the zipper as high as it would go. "Keep it like this," he ordered. "And keep your head down. The closer to the ground your head is, the better you can breathe."

"But I can't breathe!" Scoop mumbled through the wet bag.

Harley lowered the zipper. "Listen, Scoopie. The fire will be all around these rocks in about five minutes. You'll be all right as long as you stay here. Stay low and keep the smoke out of your face."

"What about you?" Scoop asked.

"I told you, I'm going around to the other side and crawl in like you did. Don't worry."

"Okay."

"And don't leave the rocks, no matter what. Promise?"

"Promise, Harl."

Harley started to pull the zipper up again, then stopped. He took a long look at Scoop's face. Reaching forward, he wiped at a smudge on his cheek. He wanted to tell him he was sorry about the fire, about a lot of things. But he couldn't get the words past the lump in his throat.

"See you," he whispered. He shoved Scoop deeper into the crack and pulled the zipper into place. Leaning on the rocks for balance, he maneuvered around to the other side. The bag dragged at him, making him want to toss it away. Not yet.

There was no crevice on this side of the rocks. Just a crack no wider than his hand. He had known this because he'd slid down that side yesterday.

He unzipped his sleeping bag and rolled it into a tight bundle. Then he cut the strap from the canteen case and tied the strap around the sleeping bag. Holding the strap in his teeth, he began climbing one of the rocks. Twice he almost fell, but he dug his fingers and toes in and kept going.

Then he was at the top. His chest hurt. His throat hurt. He struggled to catch his breath. He looked up. A few stars were visible through the smoke. The rocks stood on the only part of the island not burning. The wind was stronger here, clearing the smoke. Sparks blew around Harley's face like spring gnats.

Slowly, as if he were underwater, he untied the sleeping bag, spread it on the rocks, sat. Below him, the fire had almost reached the bushes at the base of the rocks. He prayed that Scoop's bag was wet enough. Then he curled into a ball, put his face in his hands, and wept.

10

Rescue

Harley was exhausted. His head pounded from the smoke and the flight through the fire. Dazed, he sat on his perch and watched as the crackling flames consumed the bushes. He yelled down to Scoop, but there was no answer. Maybe he hadn't heard above the sounds of the fire. Harley laid his flashlight near him on the rock and closed his eyes. He pulled part of the sleeping bag over his face. And he slept.

A noise woke him. Thunder? No, it sounded more like a motor from a boat. Someone was coming! He threw off the bag and stood. He almost lost his balance, but caught himself. He

looked around, trying to will away the smoke that shut out vision.

The sound grew louder. God, it was over his head! He looked up, straight at the underside of a helicopter. The wind from the blades whipped smoke and sparks into his face. His hair snapped into his eyes, bringing tears.

He screamed and waved his arms like a wild boy. But it was all lost in the noise and smoke. Then he remembered the flashlight. Throwing himself to his knees, he groped for the light. It seemed ages before his hand stumbled onto it. He snatched it up and began waving the light in a circle over his head.

The helicopter was no longer above him, but he could still hear its flapping sound. Yells were torn from his mouth by the wind and drowned in the noise of the fire. He stopped yelling when his throat felt raw. He waved the flashlight until his arm ached. The thudding sound grew fainter. Then it was gone altogether.

"Come back!" Harley screamed into the night. He listened, alert for any new sound. But he heard only the sound of burning wood.

"Come back, please!" he cried again. He threw his arms into the air as if trying to physically pull the helicopter back and yank it out of the sky. Crushed, he let his arms drop. Sobs

wracked his chest and throat. He gulped air as he cried. Finally, he dropped to his knees, spent.

Maybe they saw me, he thought. Maybe they'll come back for another look. He waited, staring into the smoky night until his eyes hurt. But he saw only whirling ash and heard only the snapping of things burning.

The fire had completely covered the island now. From where Harley sat, he could make out the ring of fire in the ocean: It had encircled Little Island. The rocks he sat on were the only things not burning. And Scoop. Please God, let Scoop be okay.

It had to stop sometime, he thought. He realized he had no idea how long the island had been afire. He turned the flashlight on his watch. Quarter after three. A little over two hours since he'd tossed the branch into the water. It seemed like a century.

Exhausted, he lay back down. Then, for the first time, he thought about his parents. Did they know? Had they still been awake when the ocean erupted in flames? Was it they who had called for the helicopter? It seemed much longer than twelve hours since they had packed the skiff and said good-bye.

Harley slept again. The damp sleeping bag was uncomfortable, but it kept the night air off his chest. In his dreams he was running, but had no destination.

While Harley dreamed on the rocks, Scoop slept the drugged sleep of the exhausted. Neither boy saw the fires gradually burn themselves out and die—the fire on the water through the efforts of the fireboats, the island fire simply because there was nothing left that would burn.

Harley woke with the sun warming his face. His body was stiff and shivering. When he was awake enough to remember where he was, he threw off the sleeping bag and stood up. He could not believe what he saw.

The ground everywhere was black and smoldering. Hardly a tree stood. Those still upright were charred half-trees. There was no green anywhere. He raised his eyes to see what had happened to the fire in the sea. But something else caught his attention. Half hidden by smoke and morning fog, people were moving slowly through the burned stumps and smoking ashes.

"Scoop," Harley said. It was supposed to be a yell, but it turned out a whisper. He tried again. *"Scoop! Wake up, they're here!"*

11

Going Home

The Whaler churned away from Little Island. The members of the Evans family were quiet, each with his own thoughts.

In the stern, Harley watched as the blackened island grew smaller in the distance. It was only yesterday that he and Scoop had been going in the other direction in the skiff. The skiff. He had seen what was left of it. Crushed, half covered with burned branches and soot. His stomach tightened when he thought about what might have happened if he and his brother had stayed under it.

Scoop was looking the other way, towards

Goose Island. He sat in the bow seat, enjoying the spray on his face. He was going home. For eight hours he had feared he was going to die. Now he watched for Goose Island to come out of the fog. For the first time since the marshmallow roast, he smiled. It felt good.

Millie sat amidships, where she could see both her sons. She still couldn't believe the devastation on Little Island. The Coast Guard had made them wait till the fire was out. It had seemed an eternity, instead of the six or seven hours it had actually been. Then they'd pulled on heavy boots before walking onto the smoldering island.

She shuddered, even now. Everything had burned. The small metal table was a twisted thing, almost unrecognizable. The cooler had completely disintegrated. And the boat. She had thought they might have tried to hide under it. Harley had told her they had, but then decided to try for the rocks instead. She glanced at Harley in the stern. He had a look on his face she'd never seen before. He was watching his younger brother, who sat laughing in the bow.

In the stern, opposite Harley, Peter Evans held the wheel. It was he who had bandaged Harley's arm and Scoop's head.

When the explosion had blasted the night into

pieces, Peter had given up hope of ever seeing his sons alive. There had been just too much fire.

The officer aboard the Coast Guard boat had told them it was an oil tanker. They had been tipped off that local fishermen were buying bootlegged diesel oil to use as fuel. This had been going on for over a year—until last night. Then the tanker captain and his crew were caught in the act of transferring the fuel. In the confusion, a hose had slipped, unseen, into the water. Diesel oil had been pumped into the ocean for several hours. It surrounded Little Island as the tide carried it toward shore. When

Harley threw the burning branch into the water, the oil floating on the surface was ignited. Peter almost chuckled. He bet poor Harl would never do that again.

Scoop broke the silence. "Hey, you guys. You know what? I never got to finish my chocolate cake!"

Peter and Millie made sounds of make-believe shock that he should have been treated so unfairly by fate.

"I guess it all just burned up," Scoop added.

"No it didn't, little brother," Harley said. He was blushing. "I finished it while you were getting dressed for the marshmallow roast."

They all laughed too loudly, but it felt good. Then they heard another noise. Almost a hundred neighbors had gathered on the dock and shore of Goose Island. The shouts, cheering and clapping sent sea gulls scattering in every direction.

"What are they doing?" Scoop asked.

Peter smiled. "I have a feeling they're here to see you two guys," he said softly. "Can't imagine why, myself," he added.

Harley felt a lump in his throat. His eyes were swimming at the sight of all those people yelling and waving at the Whaler. One of the kids was suited up for water-skiing. Even if Doc Thatcher said he couldn't ski, Harley was determined his little brother was going to learn. One of the other kids would teach him. This summer. Now.

7488

7488   ROY

ROY, RON

NIGHTMARE ISLAND

ST. IGNATIUS SCHOOL
10205 LORAIN AVE.